This Bing book belongs to

. . . .

The *Bing* television series is created by Acamar Films and Brown Bag Films
and adapted from the original books by Ted Dewan

Original story written by Helen Farrall, Mikael Shields and Claire Jennings

Bing and the Fire Engine was adapted from the original television script
by Rebecca Gerlings

First published in Great Britain by HarperCollins *Children's Books* in 2021
HarperCollins *Children's Books* is a division of HarperCollins*Publishers* Ltd
HarperCollins Publishers, 1 London Bridge Street, London, SE1 9GF

1 3 5 7 9 10 8 6 4 2

ISBN: 978-0-00-842060-4

Printed in China

MIX
Paper from
responsible sources

FSC
www.fsc.org
FSC® C007454

This book is produced from independently certified FSC™ paper
to ensure responsible forest management.

For more information visit: www.harpercollins.co.uk/green

Bing and the Fire Engine

HarperCollins *Children's Books*

Round the corner, not far away,
Bing is **very excited** today!

"Oh, look!" he gasps.
"I can see a **fire engine!**"

Sula and Pando
are excited to see
the fire engine too!

**HONK!
HONK!**

"Hey, Bing! Look at me!"
calls Pando, beeping the horn.
"It's *my* turn next, Pando," Sula reminds him.

Bing can't wait to have a go in the fire engine. It looks like so much fun.

"I want to sit in the fire engine, Flop!" Bing says excitedly. "Is it my turn after Sula?"

Flop nods. "Yes, I think so, Bing."

"Nee-nah! Nee-nah!"

Pando laughs.

"You can use the **real siren, Pando,**" says the firefighter. "Just press this button."

"Ohhh! That is **noisy loud!"** exclaims Bing, covering his ears.

It's Sula's turn next.
One of the firefighters
passes her the fire hose.
"Would you like to water
the purple flowers, Sula?"

"They're tulips!"
says Sula, giving
them a nice
big drink.

WHOOOOOSSSSSSSH!

While Bing waits for his turn he
tells the firefighter about his book of
Fabulous Fire Engine Facts.

"We read it
together, don't
we, Flop?"
says Bing.

Just as it's Bing's turn, the firefighter
gets an urgent call on her walkie-talkie.

"I understand," says the firefighter. "We're on our way." She turns to Bing and his friends. "I'm SO sorry. We need to leave immediately."

"Oh, but it's *my* turn," says Bing quietly.

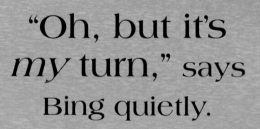

The firefighters quickly climb into the fire engine.
They put their siren on and speed away.

WWWWEEEEEEOOOOO!

"Poor Bing!" says Sula sadly.

"It isn't fair!" says Bing. "Sula and Pando sitted in a real fire engine and I didn't even get a turn!"

"You're right, Bing, they did sit in a real fire engine," says Flop gently, "but it had to go to an emergency."

"Oh no. I am . . .
disappointed,"
Bing sighs.

Flop has
a plan that might
cheer Bing up . . .

"Bing," he says, "Pando and Padget have to get back to the shop, but would you like to **invite Sula and Amma** round? We've got some **carroty bagels** at home. We could all read your ***Fabulous Fire Engine Facts*** book."

Bing starts to feel a little better. "Please. Yes, please."

On the way to Bing's house, Bing, Flop,
Sula and Amma get a big surprise.
The fire engine is parked in Bing's street!

"Fire engine!"
Bing gasps.
"Look, Flop!
"Let's go and see!"

"Wait for
me, Bing!"
shouts Sula.

Arlo the cat is stuck on the roof.

"We just can't get him to come down,"
explains Bing and Flop's neighbour.

"Come on, kitty,"
calls the firefighter. "Good kitty."

MEOW!

But Arlo is
frightened.
He backs away
from the edge . . .

Bing thinks Arlo might be playing hide-and-seek.

"Arlo! Arlo!" he calls and waves. "You need to come down!"

Sula joins in too. "Arlo! Arlo! Come on, Arlo!"

Soon Arlo feels brave
enough to jump into
the firefighter's arms.

"Gotcha!" she says as the
ladder lowers them to safety.

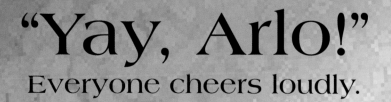

"Yay, Arlo!"
Everyone cheers loudly.

Bing and Flop's neighbour is very happy
to see Arlo and thanks Bing for his help.

"As a *special* thank you, Bing," the firefighter adds,
"we wondered . . . if you'd like to sit in our fire engine?"

"Oh! Please! Yes, please!" says Bing.

"What's it like
living in a
fire station?"
asks Bing.

"Well," replies the firefighter, "we don't live there, but sometimes we stay overnight."

"A sleepover?" replies Bing.

"Maybe one day you could come and visit? I *think* we might need your help again, **Firefighter Bing!"**

"Oh, YES!" says Bing. "Thank you!"

He leans out of the **fire-engine window** and shouts down to Flop. "Flop, can I bring Hoppity?"

"Indeed," chuckles Flop.

Bing presses the
**noisy siren
button** to
celebrate!

WWWEEEEOOOOWWWEE

"Yay!"
he shouts with joy.

EEOOOOO!

Fire engines . . . they're a Bing thing!